PURSUED BY THE MOUNTAIN MAN

MOUNTAIN MEN OF SUITOR'S CROSSING #5

HALLIE BENNETT

I0619333

Searching for *more* mountain men? Check out the rest of the *Mountain Men of Suitor's Crossing* serieshere[1]!

CHAPTER ONE

WINSTON

"**G**remlin, no!"

The cafe quiets as my Siberian husky races toward a curvy brunette and snatches the napkin-wrapped cookie from her table. A couple of customers laugh at his antics, but my wayward dog's victim isn't one of them. Instead, frown lines deepen around her mouth and eyes as she glares at me and Gremlin, who I've finally caught now that he's occupied with his sugary prize.

"Sorry about that. He's still learning his manners." *And always will be since he's a stubborn as hell husky.* But I keep that last part to myself.

"He shouldn't be off-leash in a restaurant. He shouldn't be in here at all," she huffs, picking up the ripped napkin on the floor before gathering her purse and coffee tumbler. Her slicked-back no-nonsense bun shines under the fluorescent lighting, making my fingers itch to ruffle it with my rough hands—an inappropriate urge I barely resist.

What the hell?

"You're right. But he slipped his collar and ran straight for the smell of food. Let me buy you another cookie—or two—to make up for it." Maybe she'll let me sit with her, and we can chat.

Maybe I'll figure out why my body's vibrating like a tuning fork all of a sudden, despite the obvious "leave me the fuck alone" aura emanating from her.

"That won't be necessary. I'm leaving and shouldn't have had another cookie anyway." She shrugs into a light jacket, and I take a moment to admire her lush curves before they're zipped away from view. *Damn, she's pretty.* Even if she does seem a bit uptight.

Gremlin, hungry for more treats, noses at her pockets until she skitters away and bumps into another table.

"Gremlin, sit." My firm tone registers, and he listens, but it's clear the damage is done. I should've been keeping a better hold on my dog instead of ogling the pretty girl before me.

"Again, I'm sorry. He's extra—"

"Winston! Come on, man, no dogs allowed," Caleb, the owner of the coffee shop, calls from behind the counter. Another apology's on the tip of my tongue when the woman veers around us and escapes the awkward moment. Through the shop windows, I watch her hop into a gray sedan before pulling out and driving down Main Street.

Fuck.

Gremlin and I return to the sidewalk outside Brewed, and a strange part of me regrets not getting her name or number. I usually don't go for women who aren't comfortable around animals since they're a huge part of my life as a veterinarian. Problem cases like my husky—a rescue before he came home with me a month ago—fill a lot of my time.

Women who can't handle that kind of life? They're not for me.

And this girl definitely fits the bill. She didn't greet Gremlin. Didn't even ask to pet him. So, despite my attraction, it's for the best that I didn't press for more from her.

At least, that's what my mind says.

My gut instinct on the other hand... That's a different story.

CHAPTER TWO

GUINEVERE

*W*ashington, Adams, Jefferson.

I list American presidents until my anxiety lowers, and my hands relax on the steering wheel of my car. Wednesday mornings I usually eat breakfast at Brewed because of its calm atmosphere. Not a lot of customers crowd the cafe, preferring the pastries next door at Buttercream Dreams, but that's the way I prefer it so my body's not overwhelmed by all of the noise and chaotic energy.

Unfortunately, my usual routine was demolished today by a large mountain man in plaid—because Suitor's Crossing is crawling with them—and his hyperactive dog.

Gremlin.

With a name like that, the husky had no chance of becoming anything else.

The parking lot at the animal shelter is already full of cars and buses when I arrive, and I brace myself for a hectic couple of hours. My sister teaches at the elementary school and begged me to be a chaperone for their field trip since one of the parents dropped out.

"*Please?*" *Morgan had pleaded from the end of my couch. "Think of all the cute animals you'll meet. Puppies, kittens, and we get to feed the baby goats outside. You'll be too distracted to let the kids bother you."*

It's not that I dislike children, or even dogs like the husky from this morning, but they usually run at a high-energy level that quickly overwhelms me. Give me quiet storytime at the library or a napping lapdog, and my anxiety is much more manageable.

However, my sister was desperate, and I couldn't say "no" to feeding baby goats, so now I'm here at the animal shelter praying my meds do their job of keeping me semi-relaxed.

"Guin! There you are! I was afraid you'd back out at the last minute." Morgan waves me over to her group of students as everyone waits for their tour of the shelter to begin.

"I promised to come."

Her shoulders rise and fall in hesitant acceptance as if there was serious doubt I'd keep my word. It's frustrating when my family acts like my less-than-perfect mental health somehow translates into complete incapacitation.

I see my therapist twice a month, take my meds every day, and never break my word.

Sure, I might complain about attending certain events, but I still go. Still support Morgan at the school recitals she directs. Still appear at our large family lunches every Sunday.

Fillmore, Pierce, Buchanan.

More U.S. presidents rattle in my mind as a wave of deficiency hits me. Sometimes it feels like no matter what I do, it's not enough—like no matter how hard I work on becoming healthier, it'll never overcome my family's preconceived notions about anxiety and mental health.

"Attention, everyone!" A booming male voice dulls the chatter between teachers and students. "My name is Winston Garrity, and this is Gremlin. I'm a local vet and volunteer at the shelter most weeks. While leading you through the shelter today, you'll learn about the type of work we do here and how you can help our animals. Let's get started!"

Shock courses down my spine at seeing the man from Brewed.

"Are you alright? You look like you've seen a ghost."

"Not a ghost," I say after releasing the breath caught in my chest. "He was at the coffee shop earlier and his dog stole my cookie."

"You mean that little cutie?" Morgan points to the husky who's happily receiving pets from students as everyone moves toward the shelter entrance.

"Yeah..." Gremlin is adorable with black patches around his eyes that make his face resemble a raccoon's. But based on our earlier interaction, I know I can only tolerate his high energy in small doses. And this morning? I hit the limit.

"His owner's not bad looking either." The note of interest in my sister's voice causes a strange knot to form in my stomach. Probably because she'd be a better fit than me for a guy like Winston.

Huskies require a certain kind of owner personality which Winston clearly possesses. His animated discussions with the kids as we explore the shelter showcase an outgoing and warm man, an extrovert who draws his energy from the people around him rather than letting them deplete him.

And I'm the complete opposite, unlike Morgan.

Healthier, according to my parents, due to her thinner size versus my round curves, and not needing to be on medication, my younger sister checks all the boxes a social guy like Winston probably has for the woman in his life.

It shouldn't matter to you.

My mind and body demand peace. Someone who's low-key, a fellow homebody. So why does the thought of Winston and another—*peppier*—woman leave me with disappointment?

CHAPTER THREE

WINSTON

S he's here.

I can't believe my good fortune that the girl from Brewed is on this field trip. For the past couple of hours, students and teachers alike have bombarded me with questions, occupying my attention. But now that we've ended the tour for lunch, I'm finally free to approach my mystery girl without Gremlin causing a ruckus.

He's enjoying all the scratches from the kids, giving me the perfect chance to approach her unhindered. Pausing at a bench across from her, I smile. "Hello, again. Mind if I join you?"

"Um... sure." She glances warily around as if worried Gremlin will pop up and snatch the peanut butter and jelly sandwich out of her hand.

"Don't worry. Grem's occupied with all the love he's getting from the students. Your lunch is safe."

"Oh." A short laugh brightens her features, and somewhere in my warped mind, a commitment to always making her happy crops up.

Relax. You barely know her.

But the connection I felt earlier is back and growing stronger by the second. She's beautiful in an understated way with her tight bun and modest cardigan with slacks. Our small mountain town is known for its tale about soulmates or *heart sparks*, and I wonder if they've finally found me because this immediate hunger for her is unexpected.

Especially when I don't even know her name.

"I'm Winston, in case you forgot," I blurt out as if she hasn't spent the better part of the morning trailing behind me with her class in tow.

"Guinevere."

"Like King Arthur's court."

Another grin flashes on her face. "Exactly. My mom's obsessed with his legend and the Round Table, which is why she named me Guinevere and my sister Morgan. I'm sure if we had a brother, he'd be Arthur."

"As far as stories to be inspired by, his isn't the worst. You could've been Rumplestiltskin or something equally terrible."

"True... Does Winston hold any significance?" she asks before taking a dainty bite of her sandwich. A smear of purple colors her lips until a quick swipe of her tongue licks it away. The innocent little touch brings my cock to instant attention.

"Family name." I try to clear the gruffness in my voice. Damn, what is Guinevere doing to me?

"Hee-haw!"

Guinevere's head whips to the left. "Was that a donkey?"

Great time for Felix to make his presence known. The shelter's resident donkey brays again as a volunteer leads him to a trailer outside.

"Yeah, that's Felix. He's going to a yodeling charity contest where the proceeds will be sent to the shelter."

"Yodeling for charity?" Her pretty mouth twists and tightens until another laugh bursts free. The blue of her eyes sparkles like the surface of Star Lake under sunlight, and every cell in my body hums in pleasure. God, I could listen to her joy forever.

Heart sparks.

"Will you have dinner with me tonight?"

CHAPTER FOUR

GUINEVERE

A glob of peanut butter gets stuck in my throat at Winston's question. He wants to go out... *with me.*

All the reasons I didn't think we'd work out this morning play through my mind again. Except this time, I wonder if perhaps I was too quick to judge him. It never occurred to me he'd actually ask me out on a date, yet he's waiting for my answer.

Can I let go of my fear long enough to explore whatever this bond is between us? And there definitely is one, despite being practically strangers. I couldn't focus on any of the information he shared during the tour because I was so distracted by his presence.

The whisper of *heart sparks* sneaks into my mind, but I ignore it.

"Or tomorrow. Whenever works best for you." Winston leans forward, his intense gaze heating me up from the inside out.

Oh my god, can I do this?

My nerves are buzzing with anticipation, and I've never wanted to say "yes" to something so badly. His belief that something's here overrides the doubt or anxiety I'd usually feel. It's a strange sensation—a freeing one.

So, I take the leap.

"Let's do it tonight." The words run together as I quickly force them out before my usual state of fear returns and I change my mind. A wide grin transforms Winston's handsome features from attractive to blindingly hot, and I'm stunned again that he's interested in *me*.

Did he not see Morgan?

Speaking of my sister, she bumps into my side as she sits next to me and steals a Goldfish from my lunch. Yes, I'm eating a PB & J with Goldfish, but it's an elementary school field trip, and frankly, you can't go wrong with the classics.

"What's happening tonight?" Swiping her hands together to rid herself of any Goldfish dust, Morgan offers her hand to Winston across the table. "I'm Morgan, by the way. This one's sister." Her shoulder bumps into mine again.

"Winston... Your sister just agreed to go out with me this evening."

An involuntary wince scrunches my face. I would've preferred to keep our date to ourselves before sharing it with Morgan, or really anyone in my family. They know my dating life has pretty much been nonexistent, so this will be big news when Morgan shares it with our mom and dad. Because there's no way she's going to keep it a secret.

"My sister... Guin... You two are going on a date?" An abbreviated snicker rolls through her as Morgan shakes her head in amazement. "Wonders never cease."

She could have at least pretended this wasn't a huge development. It's humiliating to have my past failures on display, especially when I miraculously managed to overcome my doubts this one time to take a risk.

Seems life wants to immediately punish me for the decision.

"Am I missing an inside joke or something?" A shadow crosses Winston's eyes as his tone loses some of its carefree personality to become more serious.

"Or something..." Morgan swallows another one of my Goldfish and shrugs. "It's just nice to see Guin loosen up a little. If you can't tell, she's a bit of a granny with the tight buns and cardigans. I've tried to convince her to stop dressing like an old maid, but you can see how far I've gotten."

"I like my hair out of my face, and the cardigans are comfortable." It's a defense I've used before, though Morgan ignores me every time. If I was one for conspiracy theories, I'd think my sister was trying to sabotage my date with Winston. But this is just her outspoken way.

She says what's on her mind—swift and blunt like a bludgeon to the head—because being a teacher requires her to hold her tongue so often in class.

"Well, bun or no bun, cardigans or not, I think you're beautiful just the way you are." The sincerity in Winston's voice causes a hot flush to rise on my skin as I duck my head to avoid his gentle gaze.

I can't believe he said that out loud. Confidently. Brazenly. Uncaring of who's around—like my sister.

Morgan snorts but keeps quiet. *Thank God.* I can't handle anymore of her commentary.

A shelter volunteer calls for Winston, who excuses himself after getting my number, and my shoulders slump in relief. Winston made me nervous enough, but having my sister insert herself into the conversation and possibly scare him off had pins and needles zinging through my veins.

It's been a rollercoaster of a day so far, and it's not even done yet. The most exciting and potentially scary part is still coming—my date with Winston.

AFTER MULTIPLE OUTFIT changes, I finally settled on a cute dress and cardigan while leaving my hair the same. Maybe I'm self-sabotaging by not doing more, but Winston seemed to like how I looked regardless. Plus, my entire style's not going to change for a man. He'll need to get used to my "granny" looks if he plans on pursuing me past tonight.

A long shot, probably. But I try not to psych myself out by thinking too far into the future.

The doorbell rings, and I inhale a steadying breath before opening the door. Winston's wearing a different plaid shirt and darker jeans while a bouquet of flowers rests in his hands.

"Hello, again... These are for you." He presents the flowers to me with a flourish, and I accept them with a word of thanks before welcoming him inside as I find a vase for the bouquet.

"This is the first time I've been to this development. Do you like living here?" He wanders around the living room, glancing out the window where there's a view of a manmade pond and gazebo.

Older residents of Suitor's Crossing opposed the development of this land for new builds, afraid it would dilute the small town's rustic charm, but more housing was necessary to keep the economy growing.

"I love it. Great amenities, easy upkeep. It was really difficult to find a home in my budget with my standards—which I'll admit were a tad luxurious for the area. These townhomes fit the bill, though. Some people complain about them, but it's right for me. I was starting to worry I'd have to move to Everton or something because pickings were so slim."

"Well, I'm glad you found this place and didn't move, otherwise we may not have met." Winston guides me toward his car a few minutes later once I've taken care of the flowers and gathered my purse. It's a shiny black SUV, and he opens the door for me like a true gentleman. The gesture makes him even more attractive in my eyes.

Settling in the bucket seat, I buckle my seatbelt and wait for Winston to start the car before responding. "True... It worked out the way it was supposed to, I guess."

"Good ole Suitor's Crossing magic at work," he teases, turning onto Avenue A before hopping onto Main Street. "Has your family always lived in town? Because I'm from here, too, and it still surprises me when I meet people for the first time as an adult rather than when we were in school."

"My aunt and uncle moved here for a job opportunity like twenty years ago, then my parents followed later during my sophomore year of high school. But I was pretty shy and kept to myself." A shudder runs through me at the memory of awkward lonely lunches. "It doesn't shock me that we haven't met before now. Morgan wasn't far off calling me a 'granny' because I'm a bit of a homebody."

Lincoln, Johnson, Grant. The names rattle off by rote. Why am I sharing such embarrassing details about myself? This is a first date! I should be trying to impress him with my accomplishments not pointing out how we obviously ran in separate crowds as teens. And probably still do as adults.

"Nothing wrong with that." Winston parks near the bandstand. A crowd of people mill around the grassy knoll in front of the large shelled stage, and confusion distracts me from the past.

"I thought we were going to dinner..."

"We are." Winston jumps out and strides around the vehicle to open the door for me again. "But a not so formal one. There are a couple of food trucks set up where we can grab something to eat before finding a spot for the concert, which should start soon. It's a local band, so I thought it might be fun to show them our support."

"Oh..." My heart plummets into my stomach. I'd mentally prepared for a sit-down meal at a quiet restaurant, not dozens of people surrounding me as loud music blares in the background. I almost want to laugh because this is a prime example of our differences—an extrovert's idea of fun versus an introvert's nightmare.

Winston studies my nervous expression. "If this is a problem, we can do something else."

"No, no... Let's go eat. I'm just really hungry," I lie. Maybe it's wrong, but I don't want to be a nuisance already. Besides, it'll probably be good for me to branch out. I like music. So what if it's outside and being shared by hundreds of people? I'm on a date with a great guy, and tonight can be the most fun I've ever had.

That's right.
Think positive thoughts.

CHAPTER FIVE

WINSTON

I fucked up.

Royally fucked up my first date with Guinevere.

Because taking us to a concert where we can barely hear each other speak? Where guests are jostling us left and right? Awful. This was a ridiculously terrible, *awful* idea.

Guinevere's uncomfortable. I noticed it the moment she got out of the car, but I brushed it off as normal nerves after she said we should eat.

Stupid.

From the little I've learned of Guinevere, she's reserved and quiet. Hell, she fucking told me she's a homebody. Yet I still thought it was a brilliant decision to bring her to a concert.

An hour passes painfully slowly before Guinevere asks if we can leave. "I'm sorry, but I've got a pounding headache. If you want to stay, I can get an Uber or something."

"Absolutely not. This is my fault. I'll drive you home."

The ride back is silent in deference to her headache. Inside, I'm calling myself all sorts of names as my knuckles turn white on the steering wheel. How did I fuck up so badly?

Honestly, this entire day I've made mistake after mistake with her. Starting with Gremlin's uncontrolled behavior around her and now this. I'll be lucky if she doesn't turn me down for a second date—something I'll wait to request when she's feeling better.

"Here we are." I pull into the parking spot in front of her light blue townhome and hurry to the passenger side.

"Thanks. I'm really sorry to ruin our date. I—"

"You didn't ruin anything. I wasn't thinking clearly about having our first date at a concert. That's on me. I should be the one apologizing." We walk up the two stairs to her front door, and a piece of paper is taped over the peephole.

"What is this?" I rip the sheet down and stare in bewilderment at the hedgehog dressed in medieval garb.

"Umm... that's probably from Morgan. She likes to drop by sometimes with pictures of hedgehogs dressed in historical costumes." Guinevere unlocks the door, and for a moment, I wonder if she's going to let me in, but she waves me forward.

"Why?" Setting the picture down, I watch as she downs a couple of ibuprofen with a bottle of water.

"More of our family's fascination with King Arthur's legend. Plus..." She motions for me to follow her to a door down the hall. It's an office with bookshelves and a desktop computer with multiple screens set up, but the most surprising addition to the space is the cage nestled in the corner.

"Come here, baby... Come on, Lancelot," Guinevere softly coos as her hand reaches into the wire caging.

"Lancelot?" I chuckle. Her family really is obsessed with the legend.

"I know, I know. But I had to keep with the family tradition." A round pointy creature rests in her palm, and she tenderly holds it aloft for me to see. "This is Lancelot, my hedgehog. He's the catalyst for the costume inspiration. Morgan's dying to see him outfitted for a mini photoshoot."

Well, what do you know?

Guinevere likes animals, after all. She just reacted like a normal person when basically bum rushed by an overzealous husky. While my preconception of her feelings towards pets clearly didn't stop me from asking her out, it's a relief to know it may not be an actual barrier to a relationship between us.

"He's a cute little guy. Who's your vet? Because I'd definitely remember you and Lancelot stopping by for a visit."

"We go to Dr. Moynahan on Hickory Street. I went to him based on reviews. Which I now realize sounds like you had horrible ones." She blushes as worry furrows her brows. "But if I remember correctly, he had the most ratings overall while also having positive comments."

Smiling in understanding, I try to ease her discomfort. "It's alright. Dr. Moynahan's practically an institution around here, so I don't blame you for choosing experience over my lack of ratings. I'll have to ask my receptionist to discreetly request reviews."

"Oh, you don't have to do that. I'm sure you're a great vet, and most people aren't as picky as me. I over research everything." She returns Lancelot to his home, and we move back to her living room.

"That's smart, especially when it comes to doctors." Scratching my neck, I catch her glancing at the clock on the left. I want to stay longer, but it's obvious she's antsy for me to leave.

Because her head probably still hurts, and you're forcing her to socialize.

"I guess I'll head out and let you get some rest. Hopefully, you feel better soon."

"Thank you, the meds should kick in any minute. Thanks for dinner and the concert," she says, leaning against the open door as I step outside.

"You don't have to thank me for that, especially when it gave you a headache. I'll see you later?" It's as close as I'm willing to get to asking for a second date at the moment. I'll let her relax and get some distance from tonight's fiasco before forcing her to decide if I'm worth another chance.

"Sure. Have a good night!"

We wave good-bye, and I drive home in a disappointed haze.

This is *not* how I imagined our first date ending.

"HOW'S MY BOY DOING, doc?" Grim rustles Tiny's ears as I type notes into his file. The name's a misnomer because Tiny is a thick pitbull with nothing "tiny" about him, but the pittie's a sweetheart and one of my favorite patients.

"He looks good. Have you had any trouble with the medication for his separation anxiety?" I ask, turning in my seat to face Grim and Tiny. They say dogs and their owners tend to look alike, and the adage proves true for these two. Tiny's bullish frame matches Grim's imposing figure while both of them share green eyes—a softening feature for both of them.

"Nah, I stuff it in a tablespoon of peanut butter, and he gobbles that shit up. No problem."

"Good to hear. Unless you have any questions for me, you two are free to go. Linda will schedule your next appointment at the front desk. See you later, Tiny." I scratch between the pittie's ears before we exit the exam room and go our separate ways.

Grim's my last appointment this afternoon, and I have plans to tackle the messy storage room before calling it a day. Empty boxes from supplies make it nearly impossible to use the room, which is becoming a problem the more the practice grows. I'm thinking of hiring another vet, which means we need more space—hence the cleaning overhaul.

After changing out of my scrubs in my private bathroom, I survey the mountain of cardboard before me. Shit, why didn't I break down each box as it came in rather than letting it pile up? This is going to take me hours to do alone.

Unless you ask for help...

It's been two days since my disastrous date with Guinevere. Surely, enough time's passed for her to consider giving me a second chance, right? But does an afternoon of labor really count as a date?

I don't want to screw up again, but for some reason, I think Guinevere might enjoy helping. It's a quiet activity giving us something to do with our hands and potentially making it easier to chat, since we'll have something to focus on other than overanalyzing what to say. Plus, it'll get her familiar with my job, show her what being in a relationship with me could look like.

Convinced this isn't a total mistake, I find Guinevere's number and give her a call.

"Hello?" It takes a few moments before she answers, and I wonder if I should've texted instead—if phone calls make her nervous.

"Hey, Guinevere! It's me, Winston. I was wondering... If you're free this afternoon, would you like to help me clear out a storage room at the vet clinic? It's mostly tearing down boxes, but when we're done, maybe I can treat you to the dinner we should've had on Wednesday."

There's a pause on the line as she considers my offer.

Come on, baby. Just say yes.

"Alright... should I bring an extra box cutter or anything?" Rustling sounds in the background as I imagine her searching for the tool.

"Sure, that'd be great. Do you need me to send the address?"

"No, I'll just find it online again. See you in fifteen minutes or so." We say good-bye before hanging up, and I notify Linda at the front desk about Guinevere's arrival. Fifteen minutes then my second chance officially begins.

Let's hope I don't fuck this one up, too.

CHAPTER SIX

GUINEVERE

The vet parking lot is empty except for Winston's SUV and an old Cadillac. It's funny how I dreamed of different dating scenarios, and all of them freaked me out in one way or another. Except none of those possibilities compare to Winston's date ideas.

But not in a bad way.

Yes, the concert gave me a headache, but his intentions were good. Sharing an activity together is like Dating 101 to help couples bond. It's not his fault he didn't realize that was one of the worst activities he could share with me.

However, tearing down boxes together? I can do that. It's simple and repetitive—the perfect distraction to prevent my mind from worrying about making a bad impression on Winston... again.

A bell rings overhead as I enter the clinic and an older woman greets me with a smile. "You must be Guinevere. I'm Linda. Dr. Garrity is expecting you, just follow me." She leads me down a short hall to an open room where the sound of shredding cardboard already fills the air. "Dr. Garrity, your guest is here."

"Thanks, Linda." Winston appears behind a stack of boxes in the corner and smiles wide as he approaches—a sheen of sweat already dotting his forehead. "Hey! Thanks for coming. I know this is a little unconventional for a second date, but—"

"It's fine," I interrupt, wielding my sheathed box cutter. "Just point me to where you want me to start."

"A no-nonsense woman. I like it." A twinkle of amusement shines in his eyes before gesturing toward another tower of cardboard along the wall. "Start wherever. As you can see, there's no shortage of work."

Snagging a box, I cut through packing tape before folding it into a flat layer and starting a pile for recycling. "No kidding. How long has it been like this?"

"Too long. We get loads of shipments of supplies—meds, toys, food, you name it. I sort out the products but by the time I'm done, I'm wiped out and just kind of shove the boxes in here for later."

I laugh at his procrastination. It's a welcome insight into his life and proof he's not perfect. Makes me feel like he's not so far out of my league, witnessing that he *does* actually have flaws. Not that this is a terrible one in the grand scheme of things, but nevertheless, it makes me feel more comfortable around him.

"And 'later' has finally arrived." My mock ominous tone draws a grin from him, and I give myself a mental pat on the back. *See? You can do this.* Just a girl and a guy on a date. Being normal and not anxiety-ridden.

Ten minutes later, we've made decent progress when Linda knocks on the doorframe. "I'm headed out, boss. Do you want me to bring in Farrah and Gremlin before I go?"

The mention of Gremlin shoots a barrel of nerves through my gut. It's not that I dislike him, but the one time we officially met he nosed all up in my personal space, full of energy.

"Thanks, Linda, that'd be great." Once his receptionist leaves, Winston turns to me. "If you're not comfortable with two dogs roaming free, I can kennel them for now. Farrah's a sweet golden retriever, and you already know Gremlin. It's up to you, whatever you're comfortable with."

I appreciate that he's asking. It's a sweet gesture. But if a relationship's ever going to work between us, I need to learn to live around high-energy animals like dogs, especially since Gremlin is actually Winston's pet. Which means I won't only see him at the clinic but also at Winston's home.

"It's fine. They can hang out with us." Inhaling a calming breath, I reassure myself this is the right decision. Even when the tips-taps of racing paws clatter down the hall. Even when the two dogs bound into the room, making a beeline straight for me.

"Gremlin, Farrah." Winston's strict tone stops them in their tracks as they stare back at their dad. It's almost comical the identical expressions of frustration in their eyes, pathetic whines coming from their throats. They're both pleading to meet their new friend—*me*.

"Sit." The dogs listen, and Winston waves me over. "I'm sure this is preferable to being jumped upon in greeting."

"Much. Thank you." Offering my hands for them to sniff, Gremlin and Farrah lick my palms before I scratch beneath their furry chins. "They really are cute. Is Farrah yours, too?"

"Yeah, she's been with me for three years. Gremlin's the latest addition from a month ago. That's why he's still a little wild, along with just being a stubborn husky. Unfortunately, his bad habits are rubbing off on Farrah. I'd hoped since she's older, it'd be the other way around, but Gremlin's too persuasive it seems."

Their sibling antics amuse me. I've never had a younger brother, but I can only imagine the trouble he gets into and how much fun it must look to poor old Farrah.

The phone rings out front and Winston excuses himself to answer it while I stay with the dogs. When they're sitting with their tails wagging, goofy smiles on their faces, it's not too difficult to fall in love with them.

"You're both cuties, aren't you? Sweet little babies..." Farrah drops to her belly and rolls over, her tail swishing a mile a minute. Accepting the invitation, I rub her belly as Gremlin tries nipping at her back legs, taking advantage of her vulnerable position.

Annoying little brother... "Grem, leave your sister alone." I playfully shove him aside, but he returns with a happy woof, lowering his front legs so his fluffy butt's in the air.

He really is cute even if he is a menace.

"Sorry about that. There's an emergency with one of my patients. Guess her kittens are coming earlier than expected and the owner is freaking out." Winston reenters the room with his vet bag in tow.

"No worries. I can stay and finish up while you handle the call."

"Are you sure? I don't want you to feel like I asked you here for free labor then bailed to have you watch my dogs, too."

Shaking my head in denial, I dismiss his concern. "It's fine. We'll hang out here while you help mama cat. It's all good."

Hopefully, it stays that way, and I'm not biting off more than I can chew.

SHOVING BROKEN-DOWN cardboard boxes under my arm, I open the back door of the clinic and maneuver around the frame, making sure to keep my body between the dogs and the outside before shutting the door and dumping the boxes in the recycling bin. It hasn't taken me long to empty the storage room of cardboard, and I'm glad I'm able to finish before Winston's return.

The dogs and I have spent the last hour together, and it hasn't been terrible. *Go figure.* Once Winston left, and I resumed demolishing the stack of boxes, they pretty much zonked out and rested on a clear patch of flooring across from me.

"Last one," I announce as Farrah and Gremlin happily yip around my feet.

Unfortunately, Farrah takes that as her cue and manages to slip through my legs right as I'm about to close the door. Cardboard crashes to the floor as I lunge for the golden retriever's fleeing form, my hand digging into the fluff of her butt.

"Girl, what do you think you're doing?" I keep my voice calm and peppy despite the adrenaline running through my veins. *That was close.*

But my relief's short-lived.

Farrah's barely inside when Gremlin sees his opportunity to escape while I'm occupied and races around the building.

"Oh, God." Securing Farrah in the clinic, I hurry to follow Gremlin, searching for his white tail waving in the wind. He's jogging down the sidewalk on the other side of the street, his nose to the ground, when the scent he's tracking veers into a crop of trees. "Gremlin! Here, boy!"

Panic surges in my heart when he ignores my call. And why wouldn't he? He barely knows me, and freedom's beckoning him on an adventure.

Winston's familiar SUV comes into view down the road. Nausea rises in my throat as I swallow the metallic flavor coating my tongue. He put his dogs in my care, and I let one escape.

How stupid!

Incompetent. Irresponsible.

Bile swirls in my gut with each condemnation. I should've known better than to volunteer to watch the dogs. Should have accepted his offer to kennel them. But I wanted to prove to Winston that I could fit into his life. Now I've only proven that I don't.

Winston parks on the street and hops out. "Hey, what's going on?"

"Gremlin escaped. I'm so sorry." *Taft, Wilson, Harding.* "I was taking out the recycling, and he slipped past me. He's somewhere over here." I gesture toward the long stretch of woods across the street. A joyous bark rises in the distance as a flash of white weaves through the trees.

"I didn't mean for him to get out. I should've been more careful. I'm so sorry." Apologies continue to spill out as we stride toward the woods. He's never going to trust me again.

Coolidge, Hoover, Roosevelt.

"Hey, it's okay. We'll find him and bring him home. Dogs escape all the time, and Gremlin's worse than most, you know that." Winston pulls me in for a quick hug before grabbing my hand in a warm clasp. "Remember, he got loose from me, too, and ran straight for you. He'll come back."

Recalling our first meeting makes me feel a little better, though shame still reigns supreme.

"Gremlin! Here, boy!" Winston calls. Another bark follows, and we head in that direction, traipsing through crunchy leaves and fallen twigs.

Long minutes pass as we shout for the wayward husky until finally he appears and makes a mad dash toward us. Winston lets go of my hand and squats down with his arms open.

"That's right. Come here, boy." Gremlin speeds forward, and I'm afraid he's going to blow past us like it's a game, but he runs straight into Winston, bringing them both to the ground as Winston gets a hand under his collar. "Gotcha!"

Relief pours over me like one of those large buckets of water at theme parks. It's a sudden crash to my overworked nerves, and I almost feel dizzy with the impact.

Thank goodness, he's alright.

The return trip to the clinic is quiet as Winston drives the short distance. Farrah barks happily at seeing us again, and Winston collars her before crating both of the dogs in a separate room.

I swiftly grab my purse from the now-empty storage room, preparing to escape as my shot nerves threaten to morph into tears. I was so scared, and now I'm ashamed, swamped by guilt and a sense of inadequacy. The same way I feel around my family most days.

"Hey, where are you going? I owe you dinner, remember?"

"Trust me, you don't owe me anything." *Truman, Eisenhower, Kennedy.* "I lost your dog, and anything could've happened to him. I should've been more careful and—"

Winston catches my arm and gently tugs me to face him. "Stop berating yourself. It was an accident, and everything worked out in the end. I don't blame you for Gremlin's actions. These things happen."

"But if I'd closed him in the storage room before going outside or—"

My words are smothered by Winston's mouth. His lips capture mine in a fervent display of control, halting my shame spiral in its tracks.

It's like the movies where the hero shuts up the heroine with a kiss, but my mind's struggling to understand this isn't a fantasy. Winston's beard really is scratching my cheeks. His tongue really is tangling with mine, tasting of spearmint gum.

Everything's very, *very* real.

And I'm stunned into submission. After two disastrous dates, he's still interested in me? Doesn't think I'm more trouble than I'm worth?

CHAPTER SEVEN

WINSTON

Guinevere's soft curves melting into my firmer body is heaven on earth. I'd acted on instinct kissing her instead of trying to talk her out of feeling guilty about Gremlin. And for once, I'm not regretting my decision when it comes to Guinevere.

All I do is mess up when I'm around her. Our afternoon started off great, but then I pushed my luck by leaving Gremlin and Farrah behind untethered. They're both rambunctious, and Gremlin's an escape artist.

Guinevere's clearly unused to dealing with dogs; she's got a fucking hedgehog, for chrissakes! So, I should've pushed to crate the dogs rather than let them roam free, since this was her first time dog-sitting.

You live and learn.

I'm just glad she hasn't pushed me away yet and told me this will never work between us. Because I can't let that happen. The more time I spend with Guinevere, the more I'm convinced she's my *heart spark*. We're different in a lot of ways, but that doesn't bother me.

I like that she's this calm oasis in my hectic world.

Here's hoping she enjoys a little chaos thrown into her *peaceful life.*

Guinevere shyly responds to the kiss, her head tilting to the side, her fingers clenching around my biceps. Tendrils of hair have fallen from her ponytail—previously as slicked back and contained as her usual buns—and the urge to feel those chestnut waves in all their glory controls my next move. One hand braces at the base of her ponytail while the other gently tugs on the hair tie until the strands are released, free to tumble to her shoulders in a shiny waterfall.

"What... What are you doing?" Guinevere rears back in confusion, her hand swiping at the thick length.

"You're always buttoned-up. I wanted to remove a little band of control." I massage her scalp with tender pressure around her temples and the crown of her head where the heavy mass of hair had been pulled so tightly. "Doesn't this feel better? Even if it's only for a couple of minutes?"

Her lashes flutter closed to rest along her rosy cheeks, and a hum of approval vibrates from her throat. "Yes... of course... But—"

"No, 'buts.' Just relax. It's safe to lower your guard with me. You've earned a bit of respite after the afternoon you've had," I whisper across her lips before claiming her mouth again in a softer kiss than earlier.

This time, Guinevere wraps her arms around my neck and hugs me close, her body stretching to align with mine. A moan of surrender emanates between us, and my cock jumps at the sound of her pleasure.

I knew my girl was hiding a well of passion beneath that reserved exterior. She may refer to herself as a "granny"—a habit

I'm determined to break—but Guinevere's far from being old and decrepit. Her body's primed to be fucked as she rubs against me like a cat in heat. Her generous tits crushed against my chest. The hot vee of her pussy grinding on the steel pipe in my jeans.

"Baby, slow down. I don't think you're ready for that yet."

"Maybe I am..." She rolls her hips and a sweet little gasp puffs from her lips.

God, is she trying to tempt me to death?

"Physically, maybe. But emotionally? I'm not sure." I hate that my stupid conscience is attempting to talk her out of letting me fuck her, but damn, Guinevere was one minute away from crying earlier because she thought she'd fucked up so badly. I don't want to take advantage of her vulnerable state. The kiss was only meant to calm her down and satisfy my craving for the time being.

Guinevere sighs, slumping a little in my embrace. "You're right. My emotions were... *are* running high. It's an odd mix of feeling safe with you while also being afraid of messing up." Her wavy hair swishes back and forth as she shakes her head in bafflement. "I felt the same way when you asked me out at the shelter, too. A sense of cautious freedom to be me."

"Tell you what, let's compromise." Gently I disentangle her arms from around my neck and put some distance between us. "Let's head out to dinner. And if you still feel the way you do afterward, then I won't refuse you. Because heaven knows I don't want to now."

"But you're being a gentleman," she surmises, a smile tugging at her lips.

"Exactly... a *reluctant* gentleman." We straighten our clothing, and she puts her hair back up, drawing a smile of affection from me. For everyone else, she's buttoned up, straight-laced. But for me, even if it's only for a few short moments, Guinevere's open and vulnerable.

I pray that never changes.

WE GO TO DAFFODIL'S on Main Street, an intimate restaurant well-known for its popularity with couples. A hostess shows us to our table near the front of the dining area, so we're able to watch those milling about on the sidewalk.

"I forgot how tight space can be in here," I say as I squeeze in between the booth and our table. This place was not made for a person of my size.

"You'd think being a mountain town they would have accounted for giant mountain men like you in their logistics."

"You'd think, but it's okay. I'll live." We order our meals, and I fill Guinevere in on my afternoon trip delivering kittens, showing her pictures of the gray and white babies.

"Oh my gosh, they're so cute."

"Well, if you're interested, I have a connection." I expect her to laugh off the teasing suggestion of getting a cat. Might be too far of a step up from a hedgehog, but Guinevere's brow lowers in contemplation as she mulls it over.

"You know, that's not a terrible idea. Lancelot could use a friend."

"I think it depends on the friend. What would the little guy or girl's name be?"

"Hmm..." Her eyes wander around the room, studying the other patrons, pausing on the mural on the back wall of old school Main Street from the fifties. "I can always use the tried and true Arthur, since we've already established one's not already in the family. However, I think that's a bit too on the nose. So I'm gonna go with... Percival."

"Who's that? I'm not up on my Arthurian legend."

"He's one of the knights of the Round Table, of course. Percy for short."

"Ahh... Purr-cival the Kitten." I joke, and Guinevere rolls her eyes good-naturedly at the pun. "I like it. Just let me know if you ever want to pull the trigger."

"I'll do that, thank you. I have to think about it some more."

"No problem. I completely understand." Not to mention, if we get together, we'll have a hedgehog, a kitten, and two chaotic dogs. But I don't say that part out loud, not wanting to scare her off by already imagining us combining our lives and pets together.

After dinner, I accompany Guinevere to her car, determined not to push our earlier compromise in case she's changed her mind.

However, it seems I'm not the only one thinking about it because she leans against her driver's side door to face me. "So..."

"So..." I repeat, letting her lead.

Guinevere bites her lip, her gaze bouncing between me and Main Street. "This was much easier in the heat of the moment."

"As most things are," I agree. "Which is why I thought you might want to wait. It's totally fine, I get it."

"Wait!" She grabs my arm as I turn away. Hope wells in my chest, but I'm quick to temper it. Maybe she just wants to talk more, which is honestly fine with me, but I don't know.

"I don't want the night to end like this," she says, and her resolve visibly strengthens as her shoulders straighten and a determined gleam vanquishes some of her earlier indecision.

"We can walk Main Street if you want."

"I was actually hoping for something more private..." Then she surprises me with an abrupt kiss to my cheek.

"Okay, I think you're gonna have to spell this out for me, baby."

"Just because we're not in the heat of the moment now doesn't mean we can't create one soon. I meant what I said earlier about feeling safe with you. I feel free to be me, to take a risk. So..."

"So..." A sense of deja vu hits as we go through the same motions.

"Why don't I follow you home, since you have the dogs to take care of and Lancelot's pretty self-sufficient."

"You're sure about this?" I double-check one more time, promising myself it's the last time.

"Positive."

CHAPTER EIGHT

GUINEVERE

G remlin and Farrah bound toward us the moment we enter
Winston's home. He'd dropped them off before meeting
me at Daffodil's for dinner, and apparently, the two hours we
were gone was enough to send them into a frenzy—acting like
they haven't seen us for months rather than hours.

"Settle down, ya hooligans. We have a guest." Winston
squats to pet both of the dogs, and I mimic his actions, burying
my fingers in Farrah's golden hair.

"Hooligans. Gremlins. You certainly call it like you see it," I
tease, my anxiety not as high after spending time with the dogs
earlier this afternoon. My body's slowly acclimating to them,
though it'll take a while before I'm ready to dog sit alone again.

Winston was kind and understanding after Gremlin's escape,
but I'd prefer to not feel that gut-wrenching fear again anytime
soon.

"Honesty's the best policy." He winks. "Let me get them
settled for the night, then we can... do whatever you want." An
unexpected flush rises on his skin, and it's endearing to see him
embarrassed. Like he's too much of a gentleman to say "then we
can fuck."

"Feel free to make yourself at home. The kitchen's through there. The bathroom..." He points out each room before leashing Gremlin and Farrah and taking them outside. Wandering the house, I debate my next move.

I've never done this before—gone home with a guy. Or had sex. Being an anxious homebody who sticks to "work, sleep, repeat" isn't conducive to meeting men or dating. Morgan might say I'm desperate and rushing into things with Winston, but despite the doubts my brain routinely conjures up about *everything*, this bond with Winston doesn't feel wrong.

We haven't had a perfect meet-cute or first date. Awkward moments have plagued our interactions, yet something ties us together—overcomes those troubled spots. And my logical mind is really starting to think it's *heart sparks*.

There's an old bridge in town where the legend of soulmates originates. Basically, a town founder and the girl he was courting crossed the bridge, and by the end of their journey, their hearts confirmed they were meant to be together. It became the courting hotspot back in the day, and it's still a popular destination among Suitor's Crossing citizens and tourists alike.

I've never been, for obvious reasons, but crossing the bridge isn't necessary to feel *heart sparks*. My friend Hannah knew the moment she met her husband, and that was during an event at the hardware store she used to work at—not on the bridge.

Then she waited seven years to act on it.

I definitely don't want to wait that long.

The thought of my life being guided by a mysterious myth or fate should probably freak me out, since it means my life's out of my control. But it's actually sort of freeing, comforting.

Heart sparks have no explanation; they just are. And you can't fight them.

Which, in theory, means I can't screw this up with Winston.

Buoyed by the notion, I step inside the master bedroom. Photos of Winston with friends or family form a collage on one wall, while frames of various animals are interspersed around the room. It's warm and homey—kind of like the way he makes me feel.

I set my flats neatly next to the door and shrug out of my cardigan, carefully folding it before placing it on Winston's dresser drawers. My hair tie rests in the center of the mossy green knit as I release my hair from the tight ponytail.

Too shy to remove the rest of my clothes and wait for Winston naked on his bed, I balance on the edge of the mattress, slightly rocking back and forth on the firm bed top.

"Sorry for taking so long. Gremlin decided he'd rather sniff the fenceline rather than piss. But everything's taken care of now. They should be good for the night." Winston hurries into the room as if he'd been afraid I'd disappear or something, and his concern cements my decision to be here.

Hopping to my feet, I edge closer to him, winding my arms around his waist. Never in my life have I been aggressive or forthcoming about my needs. I loiter around in the background, passively accepting what comes my way in order to not cause problems. But with Winston, I can't seem to keep my hands off him.

He's this burly veterinarian, a gentle mountain giant, who's my opposite in so many ways. Extroverted. Down to earth. Easy going. Not harassed by negative thoughts twenty-four-seven or by irrational fears of what could go wrong at any given second.

"I didn't mind waiting. The dogs come first."

"In this case, yes. But for the rest of the night, you're my top priority."

The promise sends a shiver down my spine. "And what's being your top priority entail? Do I get a prize?" I ask. Flirting doesn't come naturally to me, but Winston draws this formerly hibernating side of me into the light.

His rough palms slide under my dress to cup my butt, squeezing the fleshy cheeks. "More like you're *my* prize," he grunts.

"So you're an ass man."

"When it's yours." He runs his nose up my neck and nips at my ear. "With you, I'm an ass man, tit man, brunette man, you name it. And I'm a fan."

Winston's fingers hook under my panties and draw them to the floor as he follows them down to kneel before me. "I've been dreaming about this moment from the first time we met."

An irrepressible giggle bubbles out as I remember Gremlin's theft of my breakfast.

"What's so funny?"

"A dumb but dirty joke," I admit, flushing red.

"Hmm... does it have anything to do with your cookie?" The words are muffled. Winston's lips skim the inside of my thigh until his breath sweeps across my core. The shock of heat is unfamiliar but not unwelcome.

"Y... Yes..." I stutter.

Winston leans back for a moment, and the skirt of my dress falls to cover the movement of his fingers sliding between my slick folds. He watches my expression as they capture my clit, rolling it between the two digits. "You know, I wouldn't have pegged you as a woman with filthy humor. Good to know I'm wrong... Now, I have a very important question for you, baby. Are you ready for me to eat your cookie?"

Another round of giggles bursts from my chest, and I cover my eyes in flustered amusement. He's absolutely ridiculous, but I love it. It's weird laughing before sex, especially since it's my first time. Shouldn't it be more serious or something?

But his silliness makes me feel comfortable.

And really isn't that all that matters?

"Very ready, Dr. Garrity."

Winston growls at my use of his title, and in a flash, I'm on my back staring up at the ceiling as his mouth joins his hands, teasing my clit and the opening of my sex.

"Have you ever had your pussy eaten, baby?"

"N... No..."

"Now, that's a goddamn shame." His tongue flicks the sensitive button where all my pleasure seems to center. "Because you've got one hell of a pretty pussy. Pink and glossy. Sugary sweet." Winston raises his head despite my hips rising to follow his lips and meets my lust-clouded gaze. "A pussy like this?" He punctuates the point with a firm thrust of his hand, his fingers grazing my G-spot. "It deserves to be worshiped. Paid homage to every. Single. Fucking. Day."

Each word invites another harsh stroke, and my back bows at the persistent friction, the concentrated focus of his fingers on that one special spot inside me. Winston's head lowers again to suckle my throbbing clit in time with his hand.

My thighs clench around his head as best they can with his broad shoulders spreading me wide open to sate his hunger, and breathy pants fill the air as I dig my nails into the comforter beneath me. This is too much yet not enough.

"Winston... stop teasing..." I plead, helplessly scratching at his scalp, urging him closer to finish me off. This touch and go, soft then hard routine he's doing is driving me crazy.

"Or what?" he challenges. His tongue stops circling my clit to lap at the one spot that makes my body jerk in response. Instinctively, my knees draw up, my toes curl.

"I... I don't know..." You can't blame me for the lame response. My brain's mush. And really what am I going to say?

Stop teasing or else I'll leave?

Not likely. Not when he's building my arousal into an earth-shattering release.

"That's what I thought." The smugness in his tone shouldn't be so sexy, but I appreciate his confidence and know it's backed up by skill.

The cycle begins again with him layering kisses and touches on top of each other to form a confectionary masterpiece, yet each time I near release, he chooses to stop and taunt me with playful promises or crude instruction for what he's going to do next. An unbearable and wholly pleasurable experience.

Until finally Winston stops dragging out our foreplay by sucking hard on my clit, and I explode into a million pieces—my muscles clenching then softening as I melt into the bed.

"Winston!" I cry out his name, and a muffled howl follows. The forlorn melody interrupts the intense moment as we both pause before erupting in laughter.

"Oh my gosh... is that Gremlin?" I ask breathlessly, tilting my head to stare at the closed door of the bedroom as if I can see Grem on the other side.

"It's his husky howl. Apparently, he doesn't like being left out."

"I've heard huskies are vocal, but this is a new level."

Winston tenderly swipes away strands of hair sticking to my sweaty forehead and smiles. "Even for him. I've never brought a woman home, so he's probably wondering what the hell is going on in here."

"Never?" The admission surprises me. He's an eligible bachelor in a small town. Hot, kind, and good with animals—Winston's the whole package. It's hard to believe no one but me has managed to land in his bed.

"Never. Building my practice is a full time job. And when I'm not working, I spend time with my friends and family. Not searching for dates." He peppers kisses down my neck as his hand slowly caresses my arm. It's soft and calming and fatigue weighs heavy on my eyelids.

Covering a yawn, I mumble, "Except for when it comes to me."

"Exactly. Though Gremlin should receive some credit for finding you in the first place." Winston maneuvers the blanket out from under us and draws it over our cuddling forms. "Now, it's time for you to rest. You're barely able to keep your eyes open."

"But what about you—"

He wraps a strong arm around my waist and spoons my side, burying his face in the crook of my neck. "Forget about me. We don't have to shove everything into one night. I'm not going anywhere."

Silence ensues as our breathing evens out. But one question refuses to let me sleep just yet. "Do you think if Gremlin hadn't accosted me that morning, you still would've asked me out during the field trip?"

"Yes. Unequivocally yes." The emphatic affirmation settles my restlessness, and as I drift off to dream about the man warming me from the inside out, I swear I hear him add, "You're my *heart spark*."

CHAPTER NINE

WINSTON

There's nothing better than waking up with the woman of your dreams nestled in your arms. Except perhaps that woman's hand caressing your abs before lowering to stroke your morning wood.

"Careful, baby. Don't start something you can't finish," I warn, groaning at the squeeze of her palm in response.

"Lucky for you, that's not in my nature. I always follow through." Guinevere shuffles higher to nuzzle my ear, and I adore this relaxed version of her. Sleepiness still clings to her voice, so I'm not sure if it's a factor in the softening in her guard or if this is leftover from last night's orgasm. Either way, I'll take it.

My hand wraps around her smaller one to firm her grip. "Like this, baby."

A quick learner, Guinevere follows my instructions, choking my cock with the tight clasp of her hand as she uses the pre-cum dripping down the thick stalk to ease the glide of her strokes.

"That's right... Fuck, just like that..." I groan as her pace increases and her hot breath teases my ear. It's obvious she's getting off on this, too, and it's fucking sexy as hell.

Guinevere throttles the base of my cock one last time, and my release steals the breath from my lungs like being accidentally kicked by a horse. Jets of cum dampen the sheets and our bodies as Guinevere softly kisses my cheek.

Fuck, that was amazing. And I intend to return the favor.

But before I work up enough strength to roll her beneath me, an alarm goes off on the nightstand. Guinevere jerks to a sitting position, wrestling with the heavy comforter until she's free to grab her phone and turn off the blaring noise.

"Sorry, I didn't realize it was so late." The bed bounces as she gets out and starts gathering her things. Up goes the ponytail. On goes the cardigan. Her protective shields are rising before my very eyes.

"It's Sunday. You don't have to leave." Patting the warm depression she left beside me, I continue, "Let's stay in bed. I promise to make it worth your while."

Her gaze springs between me and the bed—indecision warring on her face—but in the end, she shrugs and shakes her head. "Sorry, I can't. My family has these big lunches every Sunday, and attendance is required. I've got to go home and get ready."

Plopping onto my back, I sigh, scrubbing a hand over my bearded cheek. "I understand. I'm disappointed, but I get it. Honestly, my sister and I have plans for lunch today, too. Guess I shouldn't cancel on her." Though Natalie wouldn't mind if I told her it was because I met my *heart spark*.

Guinevere pauses with one bent knee in the air as she tries to slip on her shoe. "I didn't realize you have a sister, too."

"Yup, Natalie. She's two years younger than me and teaches goat yoga."

"Goat yoga? Like yoga with goats?"

Rolling out of bed, I nod. "Yep. They're rescue goats through a program with the shelter. From what she tells me, it's pretty popular."

"Well, duh! Cute goats prancing around while you pretend to do yoga? I might have to take a class. Especially since I missed out on feeding the babies at the shelter." Guinevere finishes getting dressed and opens the bedroom door. Immediately, rustling from Farrah and Gremlin starts up as Grem howls in annoyance. He's ready for breakfast and demands to be fed now.

Bossy little husky.

"I'll sign us up. Just let me know when you want to go."

We walk to the front door—Guinevere stopping to give farewell pets to the dogs—and I can't resist dragging her close for another kiss.

"I hate that we can't spend today together," I grouse, lightly tugging on the end of her ponytail.

"Me, too." She sighs and backs away with a gentle squeeze of my hand. "But it'll just be something to look forward to, right?"

"Oh, most definitely," I promise. I'm nowhere near having enough of her, probably never will, truth be told. Guinevere's my girl—no ifs, ands, or buts. *Heart sparks* struck, and I'm not about to second-guess them.

"WHO IS SHE?" NATALIE asks the moment we sit down at the cafe table. Brewed is packed with the after church crowd, so we're lucky to have found a spot.

Turns out Linda called my mom after leaving the clinic yesterday, sharing the latest gossip about me and my mystery woman. Mom spread the news throughout the family, and apparently, Natalie's been elected as point person to suss out more information.

"Her name's Guinevere. Gremlin stole a cookie from her table on Wednesday. Actually, it was that table." I point to one occupied by a trio of older women. "Then she chaperoned a field trip at the shelter where I led the tour."

"Oh, fate!"

"For once, I agree with you. She's definitely my *heart spark*. She's sweet and reserved and has a pet hedgehog named Lancelot." A fact that still makes me smile. Guinevere and Lancelot... Guess that makes me King Arthur.

Natalie sips her iced mocha before leaning forward to rest her chin in her hand, a dreamy look in her eyes. "I'm really happy for you, Win." Suddenly, a mischievous sparkle transforms her features as she straightens in her seat. "Oh my God! Win and Guin! Can we please make that your wedding hashtag?"

Coughing on a drink of my coffee, I grab a napkin and swipe at the corner of my mouth. "Wedding hashtag? People still do those?" Crumpling the napkin in a ball, I toss it on the table. "And no, we're not gonna advertise the silly coincidence. Besides, Guinevere's not ready for a marriage proposal. I'm trying to *not* scare her off, Nat, remember?"

"Scare who off?" A familiar voice interrupts our conversation, and Natalie and I both smile in greeting as James McCoy approaches our table.

"Holy fuck! James McCoy? I haven't seen you in ages. How's it going, brother?" I stand for a hug as does Natalie. James hasn't changed much since I last saw him—he's still a fierce-looking motherfucker, but I suppose the marines will do that to a person.

"It's going well. I just came from a visit with my dad. Looks like I'm joining the family business soon."

"Really?" Natalie retakes her seat as James steals an empty chair from a couple who's leaving. "Tired of all that 'ooh-rah' stuff?"

James and I turn twin looks of reluctant amusement toward her cheerleader-like summation of marine life. "It's a bit more than a couple of catch phrases, Nat."

"No kidding, but you're partly right. I'm ready to settle down into a semblance of normal. Seeing my parents regularly. Catching up with old friends like you guys."

"And maybe finding love like Winston over here?" Natalie guesses, pulling out her phone to probably notify the entire female population in Suitor's Crossing of eligible bachelor James McCoy's imminent return.

"Have you found love? Congratulations."

"Thanks, but I'm not admitting to anything before expressing my feelings for the woman in question first."

"Smart... Well, it was good seeing you guys, but I've got to hit the road. Got a two hour drive ahead of me. We'll hang out when I return, though, and maybe you can bring your girl." James waves good-bye, and a swarm of chatter follows him as locals recognize him.

"He's gonna be a hot commodity once he moves back here," Natalie murmurs, still typing away on her phone.

"Guess someone has to take the torch, since I'm officially off the market."

"Ha! You're not the only single man around these parts, brother. Thank God." The last part's mumbled under her breath as a fake shudder wracks her body, and I know it's because she wouldn't mind finding love either.

It'll come, little sister. Just you wait.

CHAPTER TEN

GUINEVERE

Lunch with my family is a formal affair. Everyone comes dressed in their best and brings a dish for the lengthy dining table.

No matter how many times I attend—and I've been to my fair share—anxiety never fails to swamp my nervous system. It's just so many people between my family and Aunt Marie's, and they're all boisterous types who don't understand why I prefer to keep silent. Or why I feel uncomfortable around my family.

"Morgan told us you had a date this week. We're glad to see you finally getting out of the house. That's what you need more than pills." Mom butters a roll as the inquest into my personal life begins. "How'd it go?"

"Fine." Her comment about my medication rankles, but it's nothing I haven't heard before.

"Just fine?" Aunt Marie asks, staring at me from across the table. Everyone's eyes are on me, and my skin itches like I'm about to burst into flame—my temperature's rising, my heart rate increasing.

"We had a good time," I elaborate. I don't want to share more about Winston. I don't want them to pick at this fragile bond growing between us. He's my *heart spark*—I'm fairly certain about that fact. But I can't announce it to my family. They'll laugh and make me feel stupid for believing in such a fantasy.

"High praise, cousin." Aunt Marie's son, Kevin, snorts while everyone else snickers in response.

"Well, when you're ready to stop keeping secrets, we're here to listen. I swear you spend too much time cooped up in that house of yours. You've forgotten how to interact with actual people."

"Did she ever know how?" Kevin jokes again, but I ignore him. It's taking all my focus to prevent a panic attack from occurring. The spotlight on my relationship with Winston and my perceived flaws are exacting a heavy toll on my composure.

Thankfully, Morgan jumps in with tales about the field trip and all the cute animals we saw, but the damage is done.

And only increases when Morgan later leaves with me once lunch is over.

"Alright, now that it's just the two of us, spill. What's going on with the hot vet?"

It's the first time I actually have any sort of relationship news to share with my sister, so against my better judgment—and because she diverted the attention from me earlier—I open up a little.

"We've seen each other a couple of times." I leave out the part where I spent last night in his bed. Some things are meant to stay between a couple—to be privately enjoyed. "And he messages regularly, too. Earlier he sent me a picture of Star Lake and said I was more beautiful than the sun glinting off the water."

It was sweet and random and had me blushing throughout the whole drive to lunch.

"Oh honey..." Morgan looks like she's about to laugh.

"What?" Afraid of what she could possibly disapprove of.

"That's a line. And a cringey one at that."

"I thought it was sweet..." Who cares if it's corny or cheesy? He cared enough to share what he was feeling, and isn't that a positive trait?

Morgan huffs, crossing her arms in front of her chest as we stop at my parked car. "That's because you don't have experience with men."

Her words are a sucker punch to the gut. She's right. I don't. Does that mean I'm being too gullible when it comes to Winston? Doubt creeps forward.

"Look, he's the first man to really show you attention, right?" Morgan waits for my nod. "It's natural for you to go 'gaga' over every little thing because you're not used to it. I'm not faulting you for it. It's something you should've learned how to handle back in high school like the rest of us. But since you didn't, you've got to learn now."

The dig at my perpetual life as a single woman stings, especially since she makes me sound like a thirteen year old girl crushing on the latest boy band or something. "And what exactly do I have to learn? Can't Winston just be a nice guy who says sweet things? Why does there have to be a learning curve to decipher his meaning?"

"Because real guys aren't like the men in rom-coms or romance novels. Men don't text you a compliment without expecting something in return. This isn't nineteen fifty-two, granny."

"Stop calling me that," I grumble, frustration welling up under my anxiety.

"It's just a joke. Chill." Morgan ambles over to her car parked behind mine. "All I'm saying is be careful with this guy. Men who look like him aren't usually looking to settle down." *Especially with a girl like you.* She doesn't say that last part, but it's there, nonetheless.

And it confirms my worst fears.

THE NEW WEEK BEGINS like any other—I work, watch tv to relax, sleep, then do it all over again. Winston messages me in-between, but my answers have remained succinct, impersonal as I struggle to combine Morgan's advice with my own interactions with Winston.

Heart sparks *don't lie.*

Maybe when they're the real thing, they don't. But this could all be in my head. Maybe I'm imagining this deeper connection because Winston's the first guy I've actually felt a bond with.

All those feelings of freedom and peace have disappeared to be replaced by doubts and sleepless nights.

Thursday night my doorbell rings, and I carefully put Lancelot back in his cage. He's been my constant companion these past few days, cheering me up when I've spiraled into shaming myself for ever thinking a man as good as Winston would want me for more than a fling.

When I check the peephole, Winston's standing on the other side of the door, his hands stuffed in his pockets. My heartbeat quickens as sweat slicks my skin.

What's he doing here?

"Hey..." I swing the door open and gesture for him to come inside. "Where's Farrah and Gremlin?"

"With Natalie at goat yoga. Thought this conversation would be better without distractions."

"Sounds ominous." I force a smile though my insides are twisting in upon each other. *This is it. He's here to end things.*

"Sorry... I'm not trying to scare you, but to be honest, you've worried me this week. Did I do something wrong?"

Hugging my cardigan tight around my middle, confusion ripples through me. "What? No, of course not."

"Then why the cold shoulder? If things are moving too fast or you regret Saturday night—"

"No, it's not that..."

"But there *is* something." Winston searches my expression for a clue to what's going on. It looks like he came straight from the clinic because he's dressed in mint green scrubs with his name tag still attached to the chest pocket.

Would the kind of man Morgan described care enough to figure out why I've been distancing myself from him? Would he have even noticed?

Because Winston did. And the concern in his eyes is clear.

God, I've been stupid.

"A misunderstanding," I finally say, exhaling the dregs of sadness and doubt that have been my anchors this week. Morgan was wrong. I shouldn't have let her stoke my fears into a frenzy just because she supposedly has more experience than me.

Yes, Morgan's dated and had boyfriends, but none of them were like Winston or else she'd still be with the guy. Obviously, her viewpoint's skewed. And I let it affect mine.

"About...?"

"About us. Insecurity got the best of me, and I wondered if this wasn't too good to be true. Because I like you a lot, and yeah, we moved pretty fast... But it felt right."

Winston cautiously steps closer to twine his arms around my waist. "Because it *is* right. You're my *heart spark*, Guinevere. I hadn't planned on telling you until things were more stable, but I don't like you doubting me or us."

Giddy hope flutters to life in my belly, and the swift one-eighty of circumstances leaves me dizzy. "You really believe *heart sparks* are real?"

"When it comes to us? Hell, yeah. You're mine. I'm yours. Yada, yada, yada." A boyish grin teases me as he walks us backward until the back of my knees hit the couch, and we tumble into a heap on the plush cushions.

"*Yada, yada, yada*?" I repeat, laughing as he playfully kisses random spots on my face, neck, and chest.

"Yeah, you know... All the love stuff." I freeze at the mention of love, but Winston isn't fazed. "In all seriousness, I'm aware we've only known each other for a week, and it's too soon to exchange 'I love yous' according to the rest of the world. However, we live in Suitor's Crossing, a place of soulmates, so outside rules don't apply to us."

He's saying exactly what I need to hear. Maybe I should be more like Morgan and roll my eyes at his sincerity, but I'm not my sister—as everyone in my family likes to point out. I'm curvier, the anxious one, a "granny." Those things don't make me stupid, though.

My gut tells me to trust Winston. His actions prove he's not some flaky guy toying with my emotions.

"I see the wheels turning, baby. What are you thinking? Whatever you need from me to prove this is real, just say the word."

A wave of contentment settles over me as I release a calming exhale. I'm diving into the deep end with Winston but rather than a shock of icy water, it's warm and welcoming, a comforting embrace.

"You've said enough." My fingers tangle with the hair at the side of his head and draw him closer. "Now, I want you to kiss me."

CHAPTER ELEVEN

WINSTON

G *ladly.*

Our kiss is a promise. One I don't make lightly.

Guinevere's a cautious woman, but she's willing to take a chance on me—a man with crazy dogs but a heart only meant for her. Tenderness swells in my chest at the leap she's making to trust me.

Soft fingertips sneak under my top to trace my abs then higher, raising the fabric with each exploration. "Baby... you don't have to prove anything. We don't have to—"

"I know..." Guinevere continues to lift the scrub top away until it's over my head and tossed to the floor. "But I want this. Want you. I wimped out last weekend by falling asleep. I don't intend for that to happen again."

"You didn't 'wimp' out. It was an emotionally exhausting day," I argue. "You're allowed to rest. I was satisfied just getting to hold you in my arms."

She sighs, affection tilting her lips upward. "You're sweet. But that's not what I need right now." Wiggling her hips beneath mine, determination outlines her face. "I need to be yours... in all ways. No more talking. No more overthinking. Just you and me—a man claiming his woman."

"As you wish." Jumping to my feet, I secure Guinevere in my arms before hefting her into my embrace and carrying her to the bedroom I find down the hall. It doesn't look lived in with its perfectly made bed and lack of personal artifacts, but we'll soon correct one of those things.

"What are we doing in my guest bedroom?"

Ah, that makes more sense. "In case you haven't noticed, baby, I'm a big man. When I fuck you, I need enough space to do it properly."

"Oh." An adorable flush accompanies the one word of understanding, and I can't wait to reveal the spread of pink on the rest of her body. Together, we manage to remove her trusty cardigan before I whip her blouse and bra off. The tantalizing jiggle of her heavy tits being released mesmerizes me, and like a bee drawn to honey, I lower my head to suckle the berry tips.

"Winston!" A flash of pain stings my scalp as Guinevere's nails scratch at me, urging me closer, and my cock jerks in response. Pain or pleasure—I greedily soak up whatever Guinevere deigns to give me.

"That's right, baby. Scream my name. I want to hear each needy cry and satisfied moan falling from those sweet lips." Quickly, I strip the rest of our clothing away—snagging the condom from my wallet before discarding everything—and hiss when her pillowy curves cushion my thick body, our heated skin sparking at the contact.

"Damn, you feel good." Not the most romantic of declarations, but it's the best I can do under the circumstances. Rolling the condom over my aching cock, I place the tip at her wet entrance but wait before slamming home.

"What are you waiting for? Don't stop now."

"Just remembering this moment—before and after I officially make you mine."

Guinevere raises her head to kiss my shoulder before flopping back to the mattress with a soft smile. "Didn't I say something about being sweet?"

"Yeah, but I can't help it when it comes to you. Guess you're just gonna have to get used to it." To punctuate the point, I thrust deep as my fingers circle her clit, the harsh clasp of her pussy threatening to make me come way too soon.

Guinevere gasps then moans as her body adjusts to my invasion, and I'm primed to fuck every fear and doubt out of her system. We're meant to be—no matter what anyone else tries to make us think.

"Fuck! You have no goddamn business traipsing around town with a pussy this tight," I mutter, sweat dripping down my temple. "All buttoned-up with your cardigans and that strict librarian up-do. While underneath your hiding a body made for sin—*for me*—a sexy little package of silky curves and a creamy cunt."

"God, yes... Made for you..." Guinevere groans in agreement as she arches to meet each pounding stroke of my cock.

My hungry eyes study the sheen of sweat on her brow, the reddened patches on her breasts from my mouth and beard, then lower to watch the slide of my thick cock stretching the pretty lips of her pussy. Her clit's practically vibrating beneath my thumb as I feel the tell-tale sign of her orgasm rising.

"That's right, baby. Come for me. Soak my cock in all this sweet cream, and maybe I'll lick you clean after." The thought of tasting Guinevere right after my cock's thoroughly fucked her is irresistible and absolutely filthy. And I'm gonna love it.

"Winston..." With my steel length buried deep, Guinevere's pleasure bursts free, dragging me with her as I groan at the rhythmic clenching of her hot channel, wishing my cum was free to paint her with my ownership rather than fill the condom. Knowing it'll only be a matter of time before I'm fucking her raw.

Resting on my forearms, I nuzzle the valley between her breasts and press a kiss there. Guinevere's pliant beneath me, limp with satisfaction, and pride pokes its head up through the film of pleasure blanketing my body.

"Well... that was something," Guinevere finally says, tossing an arm over her head as she stares up at me with a twinkle in her eyes.

"An *amazing* something. Shouldn't expect anything less from your *heart spark*," I tease, flopping on my side and tracing her belly button.

"True. Guess I should thank Gremlin for his part in all of this, huh?"

A bark of laughter rumbles from my chest. "He'll appreciate another cookie in gratitude, I'm sure."

"Done. Although I'm going to find a dog-friendly recipe." A shadow of seriousness dampens some of her humor as she readjusts to face me on the bed. "I know we've agreed to give this thing a go, and this isn't me trying to back out. But you should know that I have limits when it comes to Gremlin and Farrah or really any high-energy situation. I'm working on it. I'm willing to stretch my level of comfort to make this work, but sometimes I may need a break from the chaos."

Grabbing her hand, I squeeze it in understanding. She shared a little bit of her concerns when we had dinner last week, and I appreciate her bravery in broaching the topic—of being honest and upfront.

"Don't worry. I get it. We'll train them together to adjust their behavior around you. They're still gonna be a lot just because of their breeds, but hopefully, once the three of you bond more, they'll settle down in your presence. This isn't a dealbreaker for me, baby. Just something we'll tackle as a family."

Guinevere smiles in relief, and I'm happy to see the tension loosen around her jawline and eyes. "I like the sound of that. *Family*. You, me, Lancelot, and two wild hooligans."

The reminder of what I called the dogs the day we emptied the storage room draws another chuckle before I capture Guinevere's happiness with my mouth.

What did she say earlier? The time for talking is over?

I couldn't agree more as I kiss my girl again, eager for our future as a family.

EPILOGUE ONE

GUINEVERE

SIX MONTHS LATER

"**M**organ was right. This is freaking adorable." The tiny medieval outfit swathes Lancelot in greens and blues, and I can't wait to see the final product of this photoshoot.

"Yeah, your sister has her faults," Winston says, hugging me from behind. "But a hedgehog in costume? That's not one of them."

The photographer Kent Moreland snaps another shot of Lancelot in all his adorableness while Farrah and Gremlin bounce around in the background. They're dressed in fake chainmail to mimic knights of the Round Table, and Gremlin's having a field day with his plush sword, wielding it around like a baton.

"Agreed. These should be our Christmas cards because everyone needs to witness this level of amazingness." Even my family might approve since it's a nod to the Arthurian legend.

Since Winston and I officially got together, he's attended several Sunday lunches with me, and each time he's shut down any hint of insults toward my weight or anxiety meds. At first, I was worried about introducing him to everyone, afraid they'd convince him of the validity of their opinions about me.

But I should've known better.

Winston loves me—no matter what. He doesn't agree with or allow anyone to belittle me, including Morgan, who's finally stopped referring to me as a "granny."

"Mmm... Christmas cards are a good idea. Maybe we can grab some of Natalie's goats, too." He kisses my temple before releasing me to wrangle Gremlin before his sword knocks out a tripod light.

A mock scolding ensues as Winston guides the husky back to his brother and sister, and Kent nods in gratitude, continuing to snap away with his camera.

I can't believe this is my life now. In love with the sexiest veterinarian this side of the Mississippi—who's as kind and gentle as he is attractive. Dog mom to two wild personalities and learning to live happily with their chaos. It's not how I pictured my future all those months ago, but this is much better.

All because a crazy gremlin snatched my cookie...

EPILOGUE TWO

SHILOH

MOM: *"Can you loan me some money? I promise I'll pay you back after my first paycheck."*

Despite the dozens of times my family's asked for money, it never fails to prick something deep inside me. It hurts every time, and instead of the pain lessening with each familiar cut, it worsens into a dull ache. Hell, my body's conditioned now, because whenever a text or call from them pops up, nausea swirls in my stomach until I figure out what they want.

Before my move to Seattle a month ago, I promised myself I wouldn't give in anymore—wouldn't enable their terrible habits by giving them money. Because it was a gift, never a loan. The thousands of dollars I've transferred from my bank account to theirs would never be returned to me.

But deciding to stop sending money and actually doing it are two very different things. And near impossible.

Guilt swamps me with every "no."

Shame sticks in my throat with every "I can't."

Maybe it wouldn't be so bad if it was a one and done conversation, but that's never how it works. My mom, dad, sister—all of them continue pushing until I change my answer, which almost always happens.

Because I'm weak. Because I yearn for their approval. Because I want to be a good daughter and sister.

Letting my phone drop to the bed beside my head, tears slip out from behind my closed eyelids. What a way to wake up on a Saturday morning. Barely conscious and already bombarded by a money request and a maelstrom of emotions.

"Get up, take your meds, then get it over with," I tell myself. Deep breath in, slow breath out. I know how to handle this. For years, it's been my normal. The only difference is now I have anxiety and depression meds, along with my therapist, to prevent me from spiraling deeper into despair.

ANOTHER WEEK PASSES before my mom contacts me again. Even though we live in the same city, we rarely see each other because I try to maintain a safe distance ninety percent of the time. It's a delicate balancing act because I moved closer to stay connected to my family, but there's only so much I can handle before I need a break.

On cue, my gut tightens as the phone rings. "Mom" flashes across the screen—a moniker that should be comforting rather than fear-inducing—and I wait for the call to go to voicemail. If it's important, I'll call her back, but if she's asking for money then I'll just ignore her. Silence over refusing her outright the safer, if cowardly, route.

When the notification for the voice message appears, I tap the bar and listen.

"Hey, it's your mom. Did you know Andi has a new boyfriend?"

No, I didn't. But my younger sister Andi doesn't tell me much about her life since it's so busy. She goes through a ton of boyfriends, works random hours when she has a job, and spends any free time hanging out with friends—to the point where she ditches plans we make together in favor of spending time with them.

The phone rings as I return her call, interested in this latest development in Andi's hectic life. Plus, it's one of the only topics my mom and I can talk about.

"Why didn't you answer earlier?" Mom asks a second later.

"It's on 'silent,' so I didn't know a call was coming in." The white lie rolls off my tongue, used to smoothing over awkward questions. My parents like to guilt trip me when I don't immediately respond to a text or don't add an "I love you" at the end of a conversation, so it's become second nature to create a plausible excuse for the "error."

Like my phone died.

Or work was really busy.

Or I didn't have time to respond yet.

Anything to prevent an extended diatribe about how their kids don't appreciate them and no one loves them, et cetera, et cetera. Because Andi's even worse than me. She's pretty much cut my parents off, making me the go-between. Their only connection to her is social media where I'm surprised she hasn't blocked them yet.

That's probably why Mom called—to ask me what I know about Andi's boyfriend.

"Mhmm... well, did you know about your sister's boyfriend? Apparently, she met him on a dating site two weeks ago. She posted this morning about moving in with him."

"What? She barely knows the guy." Switching to speaker phone, I search for his name, Andrew Gore, among Andi's friends online and immediately find his profile. Ah, blessedly public. People are too open these days with their information, but in this case, it works in my favor.

Looks like he's a marine who's a little younger than me based on his high school graduation date and the uniform he's sporting in a million photos of him with three other guys. He's attractive like a Ryan Gosling knock-off.

"You know your sister. She never thinks things through. I'm surprised she didn't tell you about him. Thought she might ask for your help moving."

"I wouldn't be able to do much with my back. Besides, he's probably got a ton of friends to haul her stuff around." Scrolling through more of Andrew's pictures, I can't help but chuckle at the injustice of it all.

Here I am—relatively healthy minus my back issues and mental health spirals, reasonably attractive if a man prefers fleshy curves, and I pay my bills with the well-paying remote job I've had for the past five years.

Yet, I've been single my whole life.

Then there's my younger sister—starting her third job this year, had her car repossessed after skipping out on payments, and couch surfing at friends' homes. But guys have flocked to her like bees to honey ever since freshman year of high school, when my dad and I caught her sneaking out of the house to meet her first boyfriend. Granted, Andi's also thin and willowy, with a vivacious personality compared to my reserved nature, but it still stings my pride.

"Well, see what you can find out about him. I don't like her living with some man we don't even know." A cheerful bark fills the background before a crumpling plastic sound hurts my ears. "I got Kiki some treats from the store today. She loves them."

Sighing, I pull up the last text conversation my sister and I had from three weeks ago when she asked me to watch MooMoo, her cocker spaniel for the weekend. "I'm sure she does... I'll ask Andi what's going on and let you know, but I've got to go now. A work email just came in."

Which is true, even if it isn't urgent. But like I said, there's only so much I can handle with my family, and this discussion is reaching the limit. Especially since it's sure to devolve into bemoaning Andi's irresponsibility.

Kiki used to be Andi's dog before she moved to an apartment that didn't allow pets. So, my parents took Kiki in rather than let Andi send her to the pound. That was two years ago. Andi bought MooMoo, another cocker spaniel, eight months ago, despite not having an official home—just sleeping at random friends' houses.

Irresponsible is only one of the words I'd use to describe my sister.

But it's funny to me when my parents want to harp on Andi's decisions as if they're not a direct correlation of their own actions while raising us. That's why I can't stand it when Mom starts in on Andi.

"Your sister never makes wise choices. Like leaving poor Kiki behind. She should've found another place to stay. If it were me, I would have—"

"Mom, I have to go. I'll talk to you later," I cut in. After all, this is a broken record I wish would break already—never to be played again.

A disgruntled huff follows my sign-off. "You always have to work. You need to take a break... Guess I'll talk to you later. Love you."

"Love you, too." Because if I don't reciprocate the sentiment, I'll hear about it.

Hanging up, I toss the phone aside and roll my head side to side to relieve the tension permeating the muscles in my neck. God, I'm so messed up. Declarations of love feel manipulative. Chatting with my mom is a chore that literally makes me sick.

And this is the real reason you're still single.

My outlook on life is skewed. My emotions are fucked up. So, I keep myself locked tight to avoid giving off the slightest signal of interest to a man. Because no one deserves to be saddled with the issues plaguing me from a traumatic childhood or the family that caused them.

DON'T MISS SHILOH AND MARINE VETERAN JAMES MCCOY IN *LOVED BY THE MOUNTAIN MAN*!

THANKS FOR READING & DON'T FORGET TO RATE/ REVIEW!

Please consider leaving a rating/review. Ratings & reviews are the #1 way to support an indie author like me.
Also, don't miss out on free books and up-to-date release information. You can sign up for my newsletter here[1].
I appreciate your support!
XO, Hallie

---

1. https://www.thearrowedheart.com/hallie-bennett

ABOUT THE AUTHOR

Hallie prefers steamy, insta-love stories where curvy girls are claimed by filthy-talking heroes. And when she ran out of reading material, she decided to write her own stories. If you want a quick, hot read, she's your girl!

www.ingramcontent.com/pod-product-compliance
Lightning Source LLC
Chambersburg PA
CBHW030356180626
46812CB00007B/2915